INSIDE MLS

SEATTLE SOUNDERS FC

BY ANTHONY K. HEWSON

SportsZone

An Imprint of Abdo Publishing
abdobooks.com

abdobooks.com

Printed in the United States of America, North Mankato, Minnesota
052021
092021

THIS BOOK CONTAINS RECYCLED MATERIALS

Cover Photo: Fred Kfoury III/Icon Sportswire/AP Images
Interior Photos: Jeff Halstead/Icon Sportswire/AP Images, 5, 7, 8, 13; Christopher Mast/Icon Sportswire/AP Images, 11; Denver Post/Getty Images, 15; AP Images, 16; Kevin P. Casey/AP Images, 19; Ted S. Warren/AP Images, 20–21, 25, 33, 35; John Froschauer/AP Images, 23; George Holland/Cal Sport Media/AP Images, 26; Leslie Plaza Johnson/Icon Sportswire/AP Images, 29; George Holland/Cal Sport Media/AP Images, 30; Rick Bowmer/AP Images, 36; Michael Perez/AP Images, 39; Gerry Angus/Icon Sportswire/Getty Images, 40; Andy Mead/YCJ/Icon Sportswire/AP Images, 43

Editor: Patrick Donnelly
Series Designer: Dan Peluso

Library of Congress Control Number: 2019954319

Publisher's Cataloging-in-Publication Data

Names: Hewson, Anthony K., author.
Title: Seattle Sounders FC / by Anthony K. Hewson
Description: Minneapolis, Minnesota : Abdo Publishing, 2022 | Series: Inside MLS | Includes online resources and index.
Identifiers: ISBN 9781532192623 (lib. bdg.) | ISBN 9781644945704 (pbk.) | ISBN 9781098210526 (ebook)
Subjects: LCSH: Seattle Sounders FC (Soccer team)--Juvenile literature. | Soccer teams--Juvenile literature. | Professional sports franchises--Juvenile literature. | Sports Teams--Juvenile literature.
Classification: DDC 796.334--dc23

TABLE OF CONTENTS

CHAPTER 1

BRINGING IT HOME

One by one, fans scanned their tickets and made their way into CenturyLink Field. Most were wearing the electric blue and neon green colors of the home team, the Seattle Sounders. By the time the players lined up to start the game, nearly 70,000 fans had filled the stadium.

The Sounders had played in front of big home crowds before. In fact, their home games often had some of the biggest crowds in Major League Soccer (MLS). This one was different, though. On November 11, 2019, the Sounders were hosting Toronto FC. It was Seattle's third appearance in the MLS Cup, but the first time the game was at their home field before their raucous fans.

Seattle Sounders fans were ready to celebrate when they arrived at the stadium for the 2019 MLS Cup.

SEATTLE SOUNDERS FC

It was something of a surprise that the Sounders had reached the MLS Cup. Two fan favorites had left the team after the previous season. Clint Dempsey, who had also been a star on the US men's national team, retired. Meanwhile, the Sounders chose to let longtime team captain Ozzie Alonso leave. They hoped to build around a younger generation of players, including forward Jordan Morris and midfielders Nicolás Lodeiro and Cristian Roldan.

But Seattle started the season well. The Sounders lost just one out of their first 13 matches. Then they managed to survive two major blows. In May, star defender Chad Marshall retired. And in August, defender Román Torres was suspended for 10 games. But the team kept rolling, all the way to the MLS Cup.

The opponent was a familiar one. Seattle and Toronto were facing off for the MLS Cup for the third time in four years. The teams had split the previous two finals, both played in Toronto.

EARLY JITTERS

The visitors controlled the action early on. Seattle goalkeeper Stefan Frei was forced into action several times. In the 36th minute, Toronto forward Nicolas Benezet had the ball in the 18-yard box. He drilled a low shot that rocketed toward the

Sounders goalkeeper Stefan Frei encourages his defenders to keep pushing.

Kelvin Leerdam fires a low shot that will deflect off two Toronto defenders and find the net to open the scoring.

corner of the goal. Frei dived to his left and stuck out his arm. He got just enough of the ball to deflect it away. Defender Kim Kee-hee then cleared the rebound out of the box, and Seattle had dodged a bullet.

Seattle did have one big chance just before halftime. Leading scorer Raúl Ruidíaz gathered a pass at the edge of the box. He shook free of a defender and faced Toronto keeper Quentin Westberg one-on-one. Ruidíaz tried to place a delicate shot, but it lacked power and Westberg easily deflected it away. The match remained scoreless at the half.

Sounders coach Brian Schmetzer stayed calm at halftime. He made a few adjustments to the team's strategy, but mostly he told his players to keep doing what they were doing and the opportunities would come. The players knew they had to step up the intensity. The electrifying crowd helped give them a boost.

MLS CUP 2009

The 2019 MLS Cup was the first one the Sounders hosted. But it was not the first one in Seattle. The game used to be played at a neutral venue. Seattle was home to the MLS Cup in 2009, the first year of the Sounders' existence. Real Salt Lake beat David Beckham and the LA Galaxy in a penalty shootout. Seattle made the playoffs that year but fell short of playing the MLS Cup at home.

Toronto started the second half by again controlling much of the possession. But once again, the Seattle defense didn't crack. It was fitting then that a Sounders defender made the first breakthrough of the game.

FINDING THE GOAL

Kelvin Leerdam received a pass at the top of the box in the 57th minute. Though a defender, Leerdam was a scoring threat with five goals on the season. This time he needed a little luck to score, and he got it. Leerdam fired a shot that deflected off two Toronto defenders. It found the back of the net to give Seattle a lead.

The goal seemed to change the game. Suddenly the Sounders were playing with confidence. They doubled their lead in the 76th minute. Lodeiro rolled the ball right into the path of Victor Rodriguez at the edge of the box. Rodriguez took a perfect strike and buried a goal.

Time was running out on Toronto. Jozy Altidore, its star forward, had been injured. However, the US national team standout was available as a substitute for the MLS Cup. His arrival on the field hardly helped, though. Finally in stoppage time, Seattle put the game away. Ruidíaz beat a Toronto defender to the ball and was in alone on Westberg. The Toronto

Nicolás Lodeiro (10) and the Seattle attackers kept the pressure on Toronto all day.

keeper had come too far out from his net, and Ruidíaz chipped it over his head. All Westberg could do was watch as the ball skipped into the net as the Sounders went up 3–0.

Altidore scored shortly afterward, but it was too little, too late. The final whistle blew, and the players and fans could finally celebrate. It was a massive moment in Seattle sports history. American football had long been popular in Washington state. The Sounders were helping prove that professional soccer could be a viable sport there too.

These Sounders had already given fans many great memories in just 10 years. But they were not the first Sounders to play in Seattle. The city's history with pro soccer goes back a lot further.

CASCADIA CUP

Though perhaps not as prestigious as the MLS Cup, the Cascadia Cup is another important trophy for Sounders fans. Portland, Seattle, and Vancouver are all near the Cascade Mountains. Soccer teams from those cities have been playing each other on and off since the 1970s. So in 2004, fans of minor league teams from each city created the Cascadia Cup to go to the winner of that year's games between them. The tradition continued with the Sounders, Portland Timbers, and Vancouver Whitecaps all playing in MLS since 2011.

The jubilant Sounders celebrate their unexpected championship.

CHAPTER 2

SOUNDERS 3.0

The first soccer clubs formed in Washington before it was even a state. In the late 1800s, immigrants poured in to the Pacific Northwest seeking work in the mining and logging industries. Many of them were from Northern Europe. They brought with them their favorite sport of soccer. Washington became the 42nd state in the union in 1889. The next year, the first known soccer clubs began to play.

But pro soccer didn't really get its start in the Seattle area until the 1970s. It was in 1973 that a group of local investors was awarded a team in the North American Soccer League (NASL). In a contest held to name the team, "Sounders" was the winning entry. The name referred to Puget Sound, a large inlet of the Pacific Ocean on which Seattle is located.

Roy Sinclair (7) of the Sounders steals the ball from Denver's Graham Bell in a 1974 NASL match.

Fans packed the Kingdome to see the Sounders take on Pelé and the New York Cosmos in 1976.

The Sounders played two seasons outdoors before moving into the brand-new Kingdome in 1976. The Sounders played the first game in the new stadium that would eventually become home to football's Seahawks and baseball's Mariners.

A passionate crowd of 58,128 fans was there to welcome them. But Seattle lost to the legendary Pelé and the New York Cosmos 3–1.

The next year Seattle looked for revenge on the Cosmos in the NASL championship—also called the Soccer Bowl—in Portland, Oregon. However, in Pelé's final competitive match, the Cosmos won 2–1. The Sounders continued to be one of the NASL's most popular clubs, at their peak averaging more than 24,000 fans per game in 1980.

The Sounders made it back to the Soccer Bowl in 1982, but despite that success, the club was losing millions of dollars. Just days after the close of the 1983 season, the Sounders folded. And after one more season, the NASL did as well.

TOP MLS RIVALRY

Nothing, it seems, can disrupt the rivalry between the Sounders and the Portland Timbers. The teams first met in 1975 when both played in the NASL. After the league folded, new Sounders and Timbers teams played in the 2000s. After Seattle joined MLS in 2009, Portland followed in 2011. The rivalry is one of the most intense in MLS.

STRIVING FOR MLS

The city was not over its love of soccer. Seattle bid for a team to begin play in Major League Soccer, the top-level US pro league that was debuting in 1996. But that bid failed. One of the reasons was the city did not have a modern outdoor soccer stadium nor plans to build one.

All was not lost, though. Seattle saw the return of the Sounders name with a new team playing in a minor league. In their first year, the new Sounders posted the best record in the league and also had the best attendance. And they were pretty good. The new Sounders won championships in 1995 and 1996.

Seattle was still eager for an MLS team. By 2002 the stadium problem was at least partially solved. The Seahawks had built an outdoor stadium. It was designed for football and had artificial turf instead of grass, but it was still a new facility capable of hosting soccer. And Seahawks owner Paul Allen was interested in owning a soccer team. In 2006 he joined a potential MLS ownership group that included Sounders owner Adrian Hanauer, film producer Joe Roth, and actor and comedian Drew Carey.

After more than 10 years of trying, Seattle finally was approved for an MLS franchise on November 12, 2007. The team

In 2007 the minor league Sounders faced MLS club FC Dallas in the US Open Cup semifinals.

Sounders fans march in unison to the team's first MLS match on March 19, 2009.

was set to begin play in the 2009 season. The only question was what to call it. The club opened that question up to fans. Sounders was not one of the listed options, but fans could also write in a choice. Most of them chose to write in Sounders. Seattle Sounders FC was selected as the name on April 6, 2008.

The rise of the MLS Sounders meant the end of the minor league Sounders. After 15 seasons and four league championships, those Sounders played their last game in 2008.

The third version of the Sounders kept similar colors of blue and neon green but adopted a new club badge featuring Seattle's famous Space Needle.

HERE TO STAY

Seattle wanted to do more than just compete in MLS. It wanted to win. The Sounders brought in talented players from the start such as goalkeeper Kasey Keller and midfielder Freddie Ljungberg, both of whom had long careers in some of Europe's top leagues. It also hired coach Sigi Schmid, who had just won the MLS Cup with the Columbus Crew. A sellout crowd was on hand for Seattle's MLS debut, a 3–0 shutout of the New York Red Bulls.

Seattle became known for two things: winning games and drawing big crowds. In 2009 the Sounders became the third MLS first-year expansion team to make the playoffs. And twice in their first three seasons they played before crowds of more than 66,000 for matches against top European clubs. For most MLS games, the stadium's capacity was reduced. But there were plenty of soccer fans to fill the place. The team averaged more than 30,000 fans per game, by far the most in the league.

The Sounders became an annual MLS playoff participant. But they found the most success in the US Open Cup. That tournament is open to every organized soccer team in the United States. The Sounders won it three years in a row, from 2009 to 2011.

A fourth US Open Cup title came in 2014. Seattle also posted the best record in MLS that year, but once again the Sounders came up short in the playoffs. It wasn't until 2016 that they broke through to win the MLS Cup. They added a second in 2019.

Ozzie Alonzo, *center*, is mobbed by his teammates after scoring the final goal of a 2–0 victory over the Chicago Fire in the 2011 US Open Cup championship match.

There was nothing minor league about the third edition of the Sounders. Their loud, passionate fans created a special atmosphere on matchday as the club established itself as one of the premier teams in MLS.

CHAPTER 3

SUPER SOUNDERS

Before 2009 the biggest signing in MLS history had been David Beckham with the LA Galaxy. The former England national team star coming to MLS in 2007 was a major step forward, showing the league could attract big names. But MLS had not yet succeeded at regularly identifying young foreign stars and developing them into superstars.

Fredy Montero became one of the league's first international success stories. He arrived from his native Colombia in 2009 at 21 years old. He'd led his Colombian league in scoring the previous two years. Montero was a star on the rise. He cemented his place in Sounders history by scoring the team's first-ever goal.

Fredy Montero quickly became a fan favorite when he joined the Sounders for their inaugural season.

US national team captain Clint Dempsey was a key figure for the Sounders upon his return from the English Premier League.

That was just one of the many feats Montero accomplished. In four seasons he became the team's all-time leading goal scorer with 60 in all competitions. Montero signed with Sporting CP in Portugal in 2013. Playing with a big club in

Europe was a dream come true for him. But fans missed him in Seattle.

Only one other scorer came close to Montero's production in Seattle. Clint Dempsey had been one of the top scorers in US national team history. As a professional he showed he could thrive in the competitive English Premier League. He brought the same scoring ability to the Sounders when he signed with them in 2013. In six seasons, Dempsey scored 47 league goals, tying Montero for the most MLS goals in club history.

Dempsey played a key role on the 2016 team that won Seattle's first MLS Cup. But a heart condition sidelined him that September, and he missed the team's playoff run. The same condition forced Dempsey to retire from soccer in 2018.

By the time of Dempsey's retirement, another national team forward was rising up the Seattle goal-scoring charts. Jordan Morris was a homegrown player in more ways than one. He was born and raised in Seattle. He played in the Sounders' youth academy before playing college soccer. After winning a national title with Stanford, he came back home to sign with the Sounders. In his first five seasons, despite missing all of 2018 due to injury, he scored 35 goals.

THE MIDDLEMEN

Osvaldo "Ozzie" Alonso had a decision to make. In 2007 his Cuban national team was playing in Houston. Alonso wanted to leave Cuba for better opportunities, but the Cuban government wouldn't let him go. So while the team was visiting a local store, he snuck away and defected. All he had with him was a backpack. His life in Cuba would be left behind.

Alonso's first playing opportunity came with the Charleston Battery, a minor league team in South Carolina. Two years later, the Sounders were putting together the roster for their inaugural team. They were impressed by Alonso's gritty defensive play in the midfield. It didn't take him long to become a mainstay in the lineup. He became known as "El Corazón" or "the heart" of the Sounders. Alonso moved on to Minnesota United after 10 seasons in Seattle, leaving a huge hole in the Sounders midfield.

Brad Evans was also an original Sounder and made 200 appearances as a midfielder over nine seasons. Evans was a great distributor of the ball, racking up 29 assists with Seattle. But he also could score himself, adding 25 goals.

Nicolás Lodeiro did not join the Seattle midfield until 2016. But by 2018 he was already the club's all-time assists

Ozzie Alonso found a home in Seattle after leaving his home in Cuba.

leader. Lodeiro signed in the middle of 2016 from Argentina powerhouse Boca Juniors. He boosted the Seattle offense right

Zach Scott—or "Mr. Sounder," as he was known—was a strong defender for two versions of the Seattle team.

away, recording four goals and eight assists in 13 matches as Seattle hoisted the MLS Cup.

SOUND IN DEFENSE

There have been many beloved Sounders players over the years. But only one earned the title "Mr. Sounder." Defender Zach Scott was more than just an original MLS Sounder. He played for the Sounders club that preceded it.

Scott's Sounders career began in 2002. The minor league Sounders players had a chance to try out for the MLS club in 2009, but nothing was guaranteed. Scott not only made the team, he played in MLS through 2016.

Chad Marshall was already an MLS legend by the time he was traded to Seattle in December 2013. He was an MLS Cup champion and two-time Defender of the Year with the Columbus Crew. Marshall accomplished both of those feats

BRIAN SCHMETZER

Brian Schmetzer has either played for or coached all three versions of the Sounders. The Seattle native was a player on the NASL Sounders from 1980 to 1983. He joined the roster of the second version of the team in 1994. Schmetzer then was the head coach of those Sounders from 2002 to 2008. He became an assistant coach when the club moved up to MLS. Finally, when head coach Sigi Schmid stepped down in 2016, Schmetzer took over as his replacement.

again in Seattle. He won MLS Cups in 2016 and 2019, and he was MLS Defender of the Year in 2014. Marshall retired after the 2019 season as one of the best defenders in MLS history.

THE KEEPERS

Goalkeeper Kasey Keller was close to the end of his career in 2008. He had played in four World Cups with the US men's national team. He played professionally for first-division teams in England, Germany, and Spain. Keller also grew up near Seattle. So when his hometown got an MLS team, he chose to sign there.

The Olympia, Washington, native got the honor of starting the team's first game in 2009. He retired from pro soccer in 2011. His final regular-season match was at home, and the Seattle fans unveiled a huge banner called a *tifo* in tribute to him. The passionate home fans in Seattle always make sure to honor their heroes.

One man was in goal for Seattle's first two MLS Cup championships: Stefan Frei. He came to Seattle from Toronto FC in a December 2013 trade. Frei immediately became an imposing presence in Seattle's net. He set the team record for career saves and wins by 2016. That same year, he had four shutouts in the playoffs as Seattle won the MLS Cup.

Kasey Keller couldn't turn down a chance to play for his hometown fans.

CHAPTER 4

MOUNTAINS OF MEMORIES

Nobody had to tell Seattle how to host a soccer match. The crowd in attendance for the club's first MLS contest on March 19, 2009, was already full of Sounders fans wearing the club's neon green and blue. They marched over to the match from a nearby park, singing and holding their club scarves. The "March to the Match" would become a regular Sounders tradition.

And their new club gave them plenty to sing about. Fredy Montero fired home the first goal in team history in the 12th minute. Thirteen minutes later, Montero set up a second goal, picking out Brad Evans, who slipped a shot under the New York Red Bulls goalkeeper's legs for a 2–0 lead.

Fredy Montero celebrates after scoring the first goal in the history of the MLS Sounders.

Seattle's Mario Martínez, *right*, fights for the ball with Real Salt Lake's Tony Beltran in the 2012 MLS playoffs.

Montero completed a near-perfect opening day in the 75th minute. He faked out the keeper and scored to finish off a 3–0 shutout. The team's performance was almost as impressive as the atmosphere at the stadium. Soccer had found a home in Seattle.

The performance of the Sounders only helped increase the popularity of soccer in Seattle. But while the team was making the playoffs every year, it did not have much success once there. The Sounders didn't win a playoff game until 2011. And it didn't look good for them the next year when the playoffs began with a two-game series against Real Salt Lake. Although they were one of the toughest teams to beat at home, the Sounders stumbled to a 0–0 draw in the first leg. But they bounced back in Utah. Midfielder Mario Martínez broke a scoreless tie with a goal in the 81st minute, and Seattle held on for a tough 1–0 victory to advance.

In the next round, with a trip to the MLS Cup on the line, Seattle was embarrassed in a 3–0 loss to the LA Galaxy. In the return leg at home, the Sounders took a 2–0 lead, leaving them a goal shy of tying up the total score. But a Robbie Keane penalty kick put the Galaxy up 4–2 in the series, and that was the final score.

CHAMPIONS LEAGUE PERFORMANCE

The Sounders qualified for the Concacaf Champions League five times in their first 11 seasons. They found some success, too, especially in 2012–13. They made it all the way to the semifinals, becoming just the fourth MLS team at that time to make it that far. Then Seattle knocked out Mexican club Tigres. That was the first time in Champions League history an MLS team had knocked out a Mexican club in the quarterfinals.

COMEBACKS

Rival Portland knocked the Sounders out of the playoffs in the second round in 2013. And not much was expected the next year, as the team lost numerous veterans including forward Eddie Johnson and defender DeAndre Yedlin. But they did have a full season with Clint Dempsey, who had signed the previous August.

Seattle soared past expectations by posting the best season in its history. The Sounders won two of the most important trophies for American soccer teams—the Supporters' Shield, which goes to the team with the best regular-season record, and the US Open Cup.

The Sounders won the US Open Cup final against the Philadelphia Union in dramatic fashion. The match was 1–1 going into extra time. In the 101st minute, Dempsey dribbled the ball up the middle. He passed it off to Obafemi Martins and got it right back near the 18-yard box. He fired a shot with his left foot past the outstretched arm of the keeper. Martins had his own turn to score 13 minutes later, putting away a 3–1 victory. It was the fourth US Open Cup title in Sounders history.

Clinching the Supporters' Shield in a showdown with the second-place LA Galaxy at home on October 25 was nearly

Clint Dempsey, *left*, scores the winning goal against Philadelphia in the 2014 US Open Cup championship.

as dramatic. It was the final game of the regular season. The match remained scoreless for 84 minutes. Then midfielder Marco Pappa, who had just come on as a substitute, buried a goal for the Sounders. He scored again in stoppage time as the thrilled Seattle crowd celebrated the first Supporters' Shield in club history.

Defender Román Torres watches as Stefan Frei saves the 2016 MLS Cup for the Sounders by tipping away Jozy Altidore's late header.

THAT FIRST TITLE

More roster changes after the 2015 season meant more uncertainty for 2016. Martins signed with a team in China. Pappa and winger Lamar Neagle were both traded. Seattle stumbled early on, and head coach Sigi Schmid left in July. To make matters worse, Dempsey was sidelined by a heart condition in August.

There were a few positives, though. Forward Jordan Morris put together a Rookie of the Year season. Midfielder Nicolás Lodeiro, signed in July, was named the league's top newcomer. They helped the Sounders make an incredible comeback, rising from last place in the Western Conference into a playoff spot.

Seattle first faced Sporting KC in a one-game playoff. The match was scoreless until forward Nelson Valdez, who had not found the net all year, scored the game-winner. Valdez, Morris, and Lodeiro were all big contributors to the team's victories over FC Dallas in the semifinals and the Colorado Rapids in the finals.

Playing in their first MLS Cup final on the road against Toronto FC, the Sounders appeared to be a little nervous. Almost all the chances in the match belonged to Toronto.

The Sounders took just three shots, compared to 19 for Toronto. And none of the Sounders' shots were on target.

But the Seattle defense held tough, and the game headed to extra time scoreless. That's when Frei made an incredible save to keep the Sounders alive. In the 108th minute, Toronto's Jozy Altidore hit a looping header toward the top right corner of the goal. Frei was moving in the wrong direction. Yet he managed to change directions and lay out, just barely getting his fingertips on the ball to tip it wide. Defender Román Torres cleared the rebound, and the game remained scoreless. A few minutes later it went into a penalty kick shootout.

The shootout was even at four goals per team when Toronto's Justin Morrow stepped up. He took his shot straight up the middle. It would have beaten Frei, who had dived to his right. But Morrow's shot was too high and bounced off the crossbar.

That opened the door for Seattle's Torres to win the game. Torres was a defender who didn't score many goals. But he did not waste any time taking his opportunity. As soon as the referee blew his whistle, Torres stepped up and rifled a kick into the top left corner of the net. He turned around and was mobbed by his celebrating teammates.

Torres calmly converted the last penalty kick to give the Sounders their first MLS Cup.

After that 2016 win the Sounders reached the MLS Cup again in 2017 and 2019—losing to and then beating Toronto FC. Seattle had a chance to win a second straight MLS Cup in 2020, too. However, the Sounders fell 3–0 to the Columbus Crew in the title game. Nonetheless Seattle had proven it was one of the premier teams in MLS. The Sounders had all the ingredients needed to remain at the top.

TIMELINE

2007

After years of trying, Seattle is awarded an MLS team to begin play in 2009.

2009

The Seattle Sounders, the third pro soccer team in Seattle to bear that name, play their first MLS game on March 19, a 3–0 win over the New York Red Bulls.

2009

Seattle becomes the second expansion team in MLS history to win the US Open Cup with a 2–1 victory over DC United on September 2.

2009

Seattle becomes the third expansion team in MLS history to make the playoffs but falls in the first round to the Houston Dynamo.

2011

The Sounders become the first team in more than 40 years to win three straight US Open Cup titles with a 2–0 victory over the Chicago Fire on October 4.

2013

Seattle knocks out Mexican club Tigres to reach the semifinals of the Concacaf Champions League.

2014

In addition to winning a fourth US Open Cup, Seattle posts the best record in all of MLS to earn the Supporters' Shield.

2016

Seattle breaks through to its first MLS Cup title, beating Toronto FC in a penalty kick shootout.

2017

Seattle reaches a second straight MLS Cup, but Toronto FC gets revenge with a 2–0 victory.

2019

The Sounders win their second MLS Cup, again over Toronto FC, this time in front of their home fans with a 3–1 victory.

TEAM FACTS

FIRST SEASON

2009

STADIUM

Lumen Field (2009–)

MLS CUP TITLES

2016, 2019

US OPEN CUP TITLES

2009, 2010, 2011, 2014

KEY PLAYERS

Osvaldo Alonso (2009–18)
Clint Dempsey (2013–18)
Brad Evans (2009–17)
Stefan Frei (2014–)
Nicolás Lodeiro (2016–)
Chad Marshall (2014–19)
Fredy Montero (2009–12)
Jordan Morris (2016–)
Zach Scott (2009–16)

KEY COACHES

Brian Schmetzer (2014–)
Sigi Schmid (2009–14)

MLS DEFENDER OF THE YEAR

Chad Marshall (2014)

MLS NEWCOMER OF THE YEAR

Nicolás Lodeiro (2016)
Fredy Montero (2009)
Mauro Rosales (2011)

MLS GOALKEEPER OF THE YEAR

Kasey Keller (2011)

MLS ROOKIE OF THE YEAR

Jordan Morris (2016)

MLS COMEBACK PLAYER OF THE YEAR

Clint Dempsey (2017)
Eddie Johnson (2012)
Jordan Morris (2019)

GLOSSARY

assists
Passes that lead directly to goals.

dribble
The touches on the ball by a player as it is taken up the field.

expansion team
A new team that is added to an existing league.

extra time
Two 15-minute periods added to a game if the score is tied at the end of regulation.

penalty shootout
A tiebreaking shootout after stoppage time to decide who wins a game.

powerhouse
A dominant team.

stoppage time
Also known as added time, a number of minutes tacked onto the end of a half for stoppages that occurred during play from injuries, free kicks, and goals.

veterans
Players who have played many years.

winger
An attacking midfielder who plays wide.

youth academy
A program run by a club to train young players and help them improve their skills.

MORE INFORMATION

BOOKS

Kortemeier, Todd. *Total Soccer.* Minneapolis, MN: Abdo Publishing, 2017.

Marthaler, Jon. *Ultimate Soccer Road Trip*. Minneapolis, MN: Abdo Publishing, 2019.

Trusdell, Brian. *Soccer Record Breakers*. Minneapolis, MN: Abdo Publishing, 2016.

ONLINE RESOURCES

Booklinks
NONFICTION NETWORK
FREE! ONLINE NONFICTION RESOURCES

To learn more about Seattle Sounders FC, please visit **abdobooklinks.com** or scan this QR code. These links are routinely monitored and updated to provide the most current information available.

INDEX

ABOUT THE AUTHOR

Anthony K. Hewson has followed American soccer since before the MLS days. Originally from San Diego, he now lives in the Bay Area with his wife and dogs.